TOAD FOOD &
MEASLE SOUP

TOAD FOOD &
MEASLE SOUP

by **CHRISTINE McDONNELL**

illustrated by **G. BRIAN KARAS**

VIKING

VIKING
Published by the Penguin Group
Penguin Putnam Books for Young Readers, 345 Hudson Street,
New York, New York 10014, U.S.A.
Penguin Books Ltd, 27 Wrights Lane, London W8 5TZ, England
Penguin Books Australia Ltd, Ringwood, Victoria, Australia
Penguin Books Canada Ltd, 10 Alcorn Avenue, Toronto, Ontario, Canada M4V 3B2
Penguin Books (N.Z.) Ltd, 182-190 Wairau Road, Auckland 10, New Zealand

Penguin Books Ltd, Registered Offices: Harmondsworth, Middlesex, England

First published in 1982 by Dial Press
This edition published in 2001 by Viking,
a division of Penguin Putnam Books for Young Readers.

1 3 5 7 9 10 8 6 4 2

Text copyright © Christine McDonnell, 1982
Illustrations copyright © G. Brian Karras, 2001
All rights reserved

LIBRARY OF CONGRESS CATALOGING-IN-PUBLICATION DATA
McDonnell, Christine.
Toad food & measle soup / by Christine McDonnell ;
illustrated by G. Brian Karras.
p.   cm.
Summary: The adventures of Leo as he tries to change his image at school, endure
his mother's new cooking, look for the right dog, and keep a lost dog.
ISBN 0-670-03509-2 (hardcover)
[1. Self-perception—Fiction. 2. Pets—Fiction. 3. Schools—Fiction.]
I. Title: Toad food and measle soup. II. Karas, G. Brian, ill. III. Title.
PZ7.M15435 To 2001   [Fic]—dc21   2001001029

Printed in U.S.A.
Set in Fairfield and Coop
Book design by Teresa Kietlinski

FOR TERRY AND GARTH

TOAD FOOD & MEASLE SOUP

CONTENTS

TOAD FOOD & MEASLE SOUP

On Sunday morning Leo Nolan was sprawled on the floor of the living room reading the Sunday comics. His father sat in an armchair reading the book review; the Sunday paper was piled in his lap. His mother lay on the couch reading the magazine section.

"That does it!" said Mrs. Nolan, closing the magazine. "I've made up my mind. It's time we changed the way we eat around here!"

Leo looked sideways at his father. Mr. Nolan raised an eyebrow in response. Uh-oh, thought

Leo, here comes another crazy plan.

"I know what you two are thinking," said Mrs. Nolan. "You think I'm going off on a tangent again, some wild scheme. You're laughing at me, both of you." She frowned, but her eyes twinkled.

Mr. Nolan smiled and winked at Leo. "Let's hear what you have in mind," he said. "We're very interested, aren't we, Leo?"

Leo nodded in agreement. Food was always interesting.

"Well." Leo's mother paused dramatically. "I think we should try something completely new. Something we've never tried before—vegetarian food. It's healthy, and it's inexpensive, and it will be a *change!*"

Bea Nolan paused and looked expectantly at her husband and her son. "What do you think?"

"Vegetarian food?" said Mr. Nolan. "You mean, no meat at all?"

"That's right. Grains and cheese and even fish, and lots of vegetables. But no meat. For a while."

Leo groaned. "No hamburgers? No hot dogs? Just vegetables?" He made a face as if he'd tasted something sour. "Maybe I'd like it if I was a rabbit." He got up and began hopping around the room, with his front teeth tucked over his lower lip. He hopped right into the side table, and the lamp wobbled precariously.

"That's enough, Leo," said his father. "You look like a buck-toothed kangaroo." He turned to his wife. "Vegetarian food, eh?" He looked thoughtful. "If you want to try it, we'll go along. But please don't do it on my account. I'm perfectly satisfied with good old humdrum American food. And don't forget those other cooking experiments you've tried. As I remember, there was a time when all we ate was French food."

Leo groaned as if his stomach hurt. He remembered the French food. All covered with sauces. Everything running together and touching on the plate. But the desserts had been good.

"Lou, you loved that French food. You always said it was delicious." Mrs. Nolan sounded insulted.

"I loved it, that's true. But I gained ten pounds. I could barely button my pants. Remember?"

Mrs. Nolan eyed her husband's waistline.

"Well, that won't happen this time. This food isn't rich. It's very healthy."

"Is it spicy, like your Chinese food? That got out of hand." Mr. Nolan made a bug-eyed face and waved his hand in front of his mouth, as if he was fanning his tongue.

Mrs. Nolan had to laugh. "Yes, I admit the Chinese food was a little too spicy."

"It wasn't just spicy," Leo objected. "It was slimy and slippery! All those little slivers sliding around, and those big mushrooms and pieces of seaweed. Dis-gusting." Leo put his hands around his throat and pretended to gag.

Mrs. Nolan patted him on the knee. "Leo, why don't you go outside for a while?"

"I'm going to rake the yard," said his father. "You can give me a hand with that."

"No, thanks," said Leo. "I'll go see if Charley's around. Maybe we can find enough guys for football."

He headed outside and soon forgot all about the threat of vegetarian food.

Sunday dinner was roast chicken and baked potatoes. Monday's breakfast and lunch were

4

just as usual: cornflakes with sliced banana, and peanut butter and jelly on whole wheat. It wasn't until Monday night that Mrs. Nolan's experiment began.

The family sat down to dinner. Mrs. Nolan dished out bowls of soup. She handed one to Leo, who set it down on the table in front of him and looked at it closely. It was reddish-brown with some chopped-up green things floating in it and some squares of white stuff too. Leo stirred it with his spoon. A few slices of carrot rose to the surface and sank again.

Leo watched as his father took a taste. He swallowed one spoonful and then another. "Delicious," he said.

Leo eyed the bowl suspiciously.

Then Eleanor, Leo's older sister, tried a spoonful. "Tastes good," she said.

Leo was still not convinced. "What is it?"

When his mother answered, Leo's mouth dropped open in surprise.

"Measle soup!" he said. "Yuck! I'm not eating any measle soup. I don't want to catch measles." He looked over at Eleanor. "You better not eat any more of that stuff, Ellie. If you catch measles, you'll be sick for Halloween."

His parents and Eleanor all laughed together. Leo didn't see what was so funny.

"It's not measle soup," his mother explained. "It's miso soup. M-i-s-o. People in Japan eat it all the time. It's very good for you. Try it."

Leo eyed his bowl and stirred the soup once more. The ingredients swirled around. "What's in it?" he asked.

"Carrots and scallions," his mother said.

"And miso. That's made from soybeans and gives the soup its taste."

"What are these white things?" Leo pointed to the little squares of white stuff.

When he heard his mother's answer, he put down his spoon in a hurry.

"Toad food!" he said in horror. "Toad food and measle soup! I'm *not* eating this. Not on your life. I'm not a toad." Leo clamped his mouth shut, shook his head, and folded his arms across his chest stubbornly.

Again his mother laughed. "No dear, not toad food. Tofu. T-o-f-u. It's something like cheese. Try it, honey."

But Leo had made up his mind. "I'll have peanut butter for dinner. The rest of you guys can eat this stuff."

Leo's father answered calmly. "Eat some, Leo. You have to try it. If you don't like it, you don't have to eat much, but you have to try a little, at least."

"Don't make me, Dad," Leo pleaded.

"Leo, stop being so silly," said his mother. "I told you. This is not going to give you measles, and it certainly won't make you into a toad."

"It can't, Leo," Eleanor added. "Because you already are a toad." She laughed at her own joke.

"Be quiet, Eleanor," said Mr. Nolan firmly. "And eat some soup, Leo."

Leo could tell that his father meant business. He dipped his spoon into the bowl of soup, raised it slowly to his mouth, closed his eyes, and gulped it down.

Surprise! It tasted good. Leo tried another spoonful. This time he kept his eyes open. It didn't taste bad at all. A little salty, but kind of nice, he had to admit.

"Not bad, for toad food," he said.

The next night dinner was something new again. Leo examined his plate carefully. On the side there were some carrot sticks.

Well, I can always eat those, he thought. At least I won't starve.

In the middle of the plate was a large round pocket of bread. Inside there was lettuce and tomatoes and crisp brown things shaped like meatballs. Some kind of sauce had been poured over the inside stuff. Leo poked his finger into the center of the bread pocket. The round balls were still warm.

"Don't play with your food, dear," his mother said.

"Mom? Do you think we'll ever have hot dogs again?" Leo wished they could have some right that very minute.

"We'll have them again sometime. But it's fun to try new things."

Leo wrinkled his nose. "Fun for you, maybe, but I'd rather eat stuff I know I like." He poked at the food again. "What is this?"

"Just try it," his mother said.

Eleanor had already bitten into hers and was chewing contentedly.

"Tell me what it is first, then I'll try it," Leo bargained.

When his mother told him the name of the food on his plate, Leo thought she said, "Feel awful."

"That's not very nice, Mom," he said. "I don't want to feel awful. If that's what this is, then I'm not eating any."

Mrs. Nolan was confused. "Leo, what are you talking about? No one wants you to feel awful."

"Yes you do, Mom. You must. You just said that this stuff is feel awful. You must want me to feel awful if you make me eat this."

Once again, Leo's parents laughed.

Eleanor rolled her eyes. "Leo, you are so *thick!*"

"I said falafel, Leo, not feel awful," said Mrs. Nolan. "It's a vegetarian sandwich. Try it." His mother was smiling and nodding to reassure him.

Leo looked at his father, who raised his eyebrows and nodded.

Leo resigned himself and took a bite. It tasted crunchy and a little bit like nuts. "Not bad," he said. "But they shouldn't call it feel awful. Nobody wants to eat something with a name like that."

The next night, when Leo came to the dinner table, Eleanor was ladling out big bowls of thick soup. Leo checked the other things on the table. At least he could fill up on bread and salad.

Tonight nobody's going to get a chance to laugh at me, Leo thought. I'm going to keep my mouth shut, that's what.

When everyone had taken a seat, and dinner had begun, Leo waited to find out what was in his bowl. But he didn't want to be the one to ask. He ate some bread and stirred the soup.

Finally Mrs. Nolan explained, "It's lentil soup. It's very nourishing."

Leo didn't say anything. He stirred the thick soup around, trying to delay his first mouthful as long as possible. Eleanor was already taking big spoonfuls. She'd eat anything, thought Leo, glancing at her sideways. When he looked up, his father was giving him the eye. Leo knew he had to taste the soup.

Lentil soup, he thought as he took a little taste. He swallowed quickly and took a drink of milk to wash it down.

"How do you like it?" his mother asked.

Leo shook his head. "I don't know who lent

11

this to us, but I hope they take it back soon and never lend it again. It tastes like mud."

Mr. Nolan chuckled sympathetically. "Poor old Leo. Looks like vegetarian food isn't your specialty. Just eat half a bowl."

Leo watched his father between his own swallows. Mr. Nolan was gulping down spoonfuls very quickly, and then taking bites of bread. I bet he hates it too, Leo thought.

That night, when Mr. Nolan came upstairs to say good night, Leo asked him, "Dad, how much longer are we going to eat this stuff?"

"Oh, I bet we all get tired of it soon. Don't worry. It's just an experiment."

His father smoothed his covers and kissed him good night. "Just between you and me, I don't like it much either." Mr. Nolan gave Leo a conspiratorial wink and turned off the light.

On Thursday night Mrs. Nolan had to go to a community board meeting. Eleanor went to glee club practice. They ate their supper early.

"Dinner's on the stove," Mrs. Nolan called as she was leaving.

Leo and his father were playing checkers in the living room. "Thanks, dear. Have a good time," Mr. Nolan called, jumping one of Leo's men with his king.

When the third checkers game was finished and Leo had won two games to one, Mr. Nolan stretched and said, "I'm hungry. How about you?"

Leo nodded. They both went to the kitchen. Leo lifted the cover and looked inside the skillet.

"Ugh! Dad, look at this."

His father peered at the concoction on the stove. It was brown, green, red, and yellow. "What do you think it is?" he asked.

Leo shook his head. "I don't know. I think it's a mistake. It looks like a messy-mushy-mix-up."

Mr. Nolan nodded gravely. "It certainly looks mysterious." He put the cover back on the pan and wiped his hands carefully on a dish towel. "How about this idea? You and I will head downtown and have a good old hamburger at the Burger Barn."

"Whoopee! With french fries, okay?"

"Hamburger, french fries, and a Coke coming up."

They walked downtown because Mrs. Nolan had taken the car. As he walked, Leo imagined the taste of the hamburger in his mouth. He licked his lips.

Leo and his father stood on line. When it was their turn, Mr. Nolan gave their order to the girl behind the counter. She was wearing a plastic hat that was supposed to look like a straw farmer's hat, and her overalls said WELCOME TO THE BARN in red letters. She repeated their order into a microphone, and in just a few minutes she loaded their dinners onto a tray.

Leo carried the tray to a corner table, being careful not to spill the Coke. Mr. Nolan carried his coffee himself because it was so hot. When they had taken their seats, Mr. Nolan reached over and tapped Leo's Coke with his coffee cup.

"A toast," he said. "To good old hamburgers!"

"To hamburgers," Leo echoed, and took a big bite. He ate slowly, savoring the taste. He was almost finished when his father whispered, "Look over at the line. Do you see what I see?"

Leo looked behind him at the counter. Standing in line was his mother!

"What's she doing here?" he asked.

"She's probably getting coffee. She hasn't noticed us yet."

The line moved forward until Mrs. Nolan stood at the counter. She gave her order to the girl. Leo watched, expecting the girl to put a cup of coffee on his mother's tray. She did, but she also put on something else.

"Dad, look! Mom's buying a cheeseburger!"

Mr. Nolan chuckled. "Looks like we're not the only ones who are tired of vegetables."

He walked up to the counter and picked up Mrs. Nolan's tray while she was paying for the food. They were both smiling when they reached the table.

"I'm surprised to see you here," said Mrs. Nolan.

"*You're* surprised? Imagine how we felt when we saw you standing in line," said Mr. Nolan.

"Mom, you're eating a cheeseburger!" said Leo.

His mother looked down at her plate sheepishly. "Yes. It's exactly what I wanted."

"It's just what we wanted too," said Leo.

"I guess we're all tired of vegetarian food," said Mrs. Nolan. "Too much of anything gets boring."

"That's true," said Mr. Nolan. "Too much of anything. Even cooking. I've been thinking about it. How about if the kids and I take over the cooking for a while? We can do it."

Mrs. Nolan looked at her husband in surprise. "Do you think you could?" She sounded very hopeful.

"Sure! The kids will help me. Won't you, Leo?"

Leo nodded enthusiastically.

Mrs. Nolan smiled and sighed. "I *am* tired of cooking." She took a bite out of her cheeseburger. "I like vegetarian food, but not all the time. And I have to agree, this tastes better than toad food and measle soup."

Leo finished his hamburger and took a gulp of Coke. No more strange food. At least not for a while. He imagined himself in the kitchen with a big apron on. Maybe Dad will get me a chef's hat, he thought.

"You know what I'm going to make when it's my turn to cook?"

"No. What?" asked his father.

Leo smiled slyly before he answered. "Chicken-pox pies!"

BOOK REPORT DAY

Leo was sitting with his friends Ivy and Will during lunch. The cafeteria rang with laughter and talking and the clatter of plates and trays. The children had to shout in order to be heard.

"I'm going to be Pippi," Ivy said.

"What?" Leo was confused. He hadn't been listening to the conversation. Instead, he had been trying to turn his entire carton of milk into bubbles by blowing into it with his straw.

"I'm going to be Pippi Longstocking for Book Report Day," Ivy repeated. "I made a wig out of orange yarn."

Leo had forgotten all about Book Report Day.

"I'm coming as Willie Mays," said Will. "I got a biography out on him. You know, my dad named me after Willie Mays."

Leo nodded. Will had told him that at least ten times before. Even so, Will had a good idea. He could just wear his Little League uniform and carry a glove for his costume.

"When is Book Report Day?" Leo asked.

"Next Friday. Did you forget?"

Leo nodded glumly.

"I better go to the library this afternoon. Tell the guys I won't be able to play, okay, Will?"

After school Leo headed for the library before going home. He ran the whole way. At the top of the front stairs he leaned against a column and paused to catch his breath.

He thought about the assignment. Mrs. Wilson had announced it weeks ago, but he hadn't paid much attention. It had seemed so far away then. Now it was just next week. A book report in costume. Everyone had to come dressed as a character. You had to stand up and tell about your book dressed in a costume. Leo shuddered. He hated standing up in front of the class. Last year he hadn't minded. He liked being a clown last year. He used to say silly things and he didn't mind if people laughed. But that was last year.

This year he was older. He wasn't a clown anymore. Or at least he didn't want to be one. But every time he had to stand up in front of the class, everyone laughed. Maybe they laughed because they were used to laughing last year. Whatever the reason, Leo wished they'd stop.

He pushed open the heavy wooden door and went inside. The library was warm and quiet. It smelled of floor polish and old books—a sweet, dry, lemony smell that made Leo feel calm and relaxed.

He turned right in the main hall and went into the children's section, a big sunny room with bookshelves all around the edges. Tables stood in every corner, and there was a carpeted reading nook where you could climb up and sprawl back on a pillow.

Mrs. Hutchins, the librarian, was sitting at her desk in the middle of the room helping a second-grader with her spelling homework. The girl was chewing on the end of her braid as she thought of the correct letters. Her braids reminded Leo of Ivy's book report character, Pippi.

Mrs. Hutchins greeted Leo with a big smile. "Why, hello! I haven't seen you for some time. You must be busy playing football."

"How did you know?"

"Oh, it wasn't hard to guess. I haven't seen Will or Charley lately either. And football is the usual activity in the fall. What brings you in here on a bright afternoon?"

"I need a book for a book report," Leo answered, sounding very unenthusiastic.

Mrs. Hutchins gave the speller back to its owner and stood up. She led Leo over to the fiction shelves.

"You're interested in space, aren't you, Leo?"

He nodded.

She handed him a book with a rocket ship on the cover and another showing two robots walking across a moonscape. They looked interesting, but Leo didn't want to go to school dressed like a spaceman or a robot. First of all, the older guys on his block would tease him. He could hear them now. Bulldog Nelson would probably call him something like "Moon Goon." Then at school there would be even more fuss. It would be too embarrassing to go in such a noticeable costume.

Next Mrs. Hutchins gave Leo a book with a cover showing a mouse dressed up like a pirate. It was a story about some mice who go aboard the wrong ship and, by mistake, go to sea with pirates who are on a treasure hunt. Leo guessed that the mice would probably have a part in finding the treasure. He put the book on top of the pile even though he knew for sure that he would never be willing to go to school dressed up as a mouse.

The other books that Mrs. Hutchins gave Leo sounded good too. But they all featured unusual characters—beavers, rats, rabbits, Martians, little people, elves, or children from other countries like Japan or Africa.

"Thanks a lot, Mrs. Hutchins," Leo said finally. "I'll look these over."

He sat down at a round table and went through the stack. Every single book would need a special costume. Some were impossible. How could he ever turn into a Borrower? They were only a few inches tall. He didn't want to go as a cat or a mouse or a cricket. Cats and mice were kindergarten costumes, and a cricket would be too hard. A cricket would be one ugly costume, though, Leo thought. A giant cricket with a shiny black shell. Not bad. Pretty disgusting. But it would be hard to make, and there wasn't much time. Besides, kids might laugh, even though it was ugly. If only he could think of a character that didn't need much of a costume.

The very best character, Leo decided, would be just an ordinary kid. Maybe looking just a little bit different. Carrying or wearing something that identified him. But nothing too fancy.

Leo stacked the books carefully on the table and went back to the librarian's desk.

"No luck, Leo?"

Leo shook his head. "Mrs. Hutchins, this isn't an ordinary book report I have to do. It's different. I have to dress up like one of the characters."

"Oh, a costume book report. That sounds like fun."

Leo sighed. Everyone thought it sounded like fun except him.

"But, Mrs. Hutchins, I'm kind of late. I don't have time to make a fancy costume. I hardly have enough time to read the book."

The librarian nodded sympathetically. I bet she hears this all the time, Leo thought.

He continued. "Do you think you could show me a book about a regular person? A boy? Maybe a funny book? And not too long?"

"A thin funny book about a boy? I think we can find what you're looking for."

She walked briskly in front of the shelves, stopping three times to pick out a book. They didn't look especially thin to Leo. Mrs. Hutchins handed him the books and said, "Look these over and see what you think."

Leo sat down at the table again and began to leaf through the first book. Then he noticed the clock on the wall. It was almost five, and he hadn't told his mother where he was. He quickly pulled on his jacket and tucked the three books under his arm.

"Thanks, Mrs. Hutchins. I'm taking all three."

He checked them out and headed home at a fast trot.

Over the next few days Leo looked carefully through all three books. The first was about a boy detective. He didn't wear anything special or carry anything unusual. In fact, there wasn't anything that Leo could think of that would make a costume. He was ordinary, all right. Too ordinary. Detectives have to be like that to blend in.

The second book character was ordinary too. But he had a dog. In one episode the boy carried his dog home in a box. But Leo knew he couldn't take a dog to school. Not even in a box. Not without getting into trouble.

The third book was also about a boy. He looked like a nice kid. Someone you would like to have for a friend. His name was Homer Price. That was the name of the book too. Homer Price sauntered along with his hands in his pockets. He had a lot of adventures. One time he caught some thieves, and another time he made a mistake with his uncle's doughnut machine. Thousands of doughnuts came pouring out. That was Leo's favorite part. Poor Homer Price. Doughnuts everywhere.

How can I look like Homer Price? Leo wondered. He studied the illustrations in the book, but he couldn't decide what his costume should be. Book Report Day was only two days away.

It wasn't until Thursday afternoon that Leo finally figured out how he could be Homer Price. The idea came to him as he was walking home from school.

The walk took Leo through the tunnel under the railroad tracks, past a drugstore where he sometimes bought candy, past a dress shop and a vegetable stand. Then there were two gas stations, right next to each other. After that came the pet store, the cleaners, and a bookstore. And then, right on the corner with the traffic light, stood the bakery, Dee Dee's.

Leo stopped to look in the window. There were two pies and a chocolate cake on a stand in the corner, and right in front were a tray of powdered doughnuts, a tray of glazed doughnuts, and a tray of chocolate doughnuts. The doughnuts reminded him of Homer Price. Suddenly he knew just what to do!

He checked the price list. If he used all of his saved-up allowance, he could buy two dozen doughnuts. That would be enough for everyone in the class. He smiled at his reflection in the bakery window. His problem was solved. He stuck his hands in his pockets, just like Homer Price, and whistled all the way home.

On Friday, Book Report Day, Leo woke up and got dressed just the way he did every school day. The only thing he did differently was to tuck his savings safely into his back pocket. He also remembered to put *Homer Price* in his knapsack. He raced through breakfast so he would have plenty of time to stop at Dee Dee's. But it was crowded in Dee Dee's, so even though he had started early, Leo reached school after the bell had rung.

Everyone was already inside. Leo walked quickly through the empty halls. From each classroom he could hear the sounds of the school day starting. "Take out your pencils . . ." "Who can tell me the name . . ." "One person at each table collect the workbooks . . ." "Now, boys and girls . . ."

Leo turned the corner at the end of the hall and pushed open the door to Room 16. Mrs. Wilson was sitting at her desk speaking to the class. She turned and paused as Leo came in, raising her eyebrows in disapproval.

I bet she thinks I don't have a costume, Leo thought as he walked to his desk.

Ivy gave him a welcoming poke as he passed by her seat. Her orange Pippi braids stuck out from her head at funny angles. From the other side of the room Will waved his glove a little. He was wearing his Little League uniform.

Leo looked around. Not everyone had worn a costume. Over in the corner by the flag there was a pile of boxes and shopping bags with things like telltale wings sticking out, and even a fat green tail showing. And leaning against the blackboard was a round white thing that looked like half a giant tennis ball.

Leo carefully placed his boxes under his chair and listened to Mrs. Wilson.

"First we'll do arithmetic and check our geography workbooks. Then we will have our reading groups. I've arranged for us to eat early so we'll have plenty of time for our book reports. After lunch we'll put on our costumes here in the classroom. Then we will all go down to the auditorium. We'll be using the stage for the book reports."

Leo rested his chin on his hands. It was bad enough to stand up in front of the classroom. To stand up on the stage would be even worse. Everyone else seemed excited by the idea. I wish I'd come as a ghost, Leo thought. Then I'd walk up on the stage and disappear behind the curtain. I'd pretend to be invisible. Nobody would be able to find me. I'd sneak out the back window and run home. Oh, well, he sighed to himself. By three o'clock it will all be over.

The morning went by in a flash. Before Leo knew it, the class was heading down to lunch.

"Is that your costume in those boxes under your chair?" Ivy asked.

"Sort of," said Leo. After all, it wasn't really a costume. It wasn't something that you wore.

Ivy had drawn big dark freckles on her nose. "I used my mother's eyebrow pencil. I hope I win a prize."

Leo didn't care if he won anything. He just wanted to get it over with.

Back in the classroom everyone scurried around putting on costumes. Most people put them on over their regular clothes. But a few of the girls had to change. They made a big deal about needing a private place so no one would see their underwear. Mrs. Wilson let them change in the girls' bathroom.

The green tail that had been sticking out of the bag in the corner belonged to a bright-green dragon. The big white thing shaped like half a giant tennis ball turned out to be an enormous egg. The wings belonged to The Littlest Angel, who was standing next to a boy wearing a store-bought Robin Hood costume.

That's almost like cheating, thought Leo when he noticed Robin Hood.

Ivy and Will were already in costume. They stopped by Leo's desk.

"Aren't you going to change?" Ivy asked.

Leo shook his head.

"You'll get in trouble," she warned. "Everyone has to be in costume."

Will nodded in agreement.

"I don't need a costume to be my character," Leo explained. "You'll see." He tried to sound confident but he felt nervous. What if Mrs. Wilson didn't accept his version of a costume? Maybe she would think he was trying to get out of doing the assignment. Leo hugged the doughnut boxes to his chest. It was too late to change his mind. He'd have to go through with it. He wished he'd brought something to wear. If only he had thought of bringing an apron. Then he would look like a baker. Did Homer Price wear an apron? He couldn't remember.

"I know that you are all very excited," Mrs. Wilson said in a deliberately calm voice. "But please remember that the other classes are busy with lessons and should not be disturbed. I want you to walk down to the auditorium as quietly as possible."

They did try to walk quietly, but one boy got the hiccups from excitement, and two other children got the giggles. Little snorts and chuckles escaped. Socks slipped on the wooden floor, and children pretended to be skating. Finally they reached the auditorium and raced down the aisles, vying for the best seats.

"Everyone take a seat. That is, everyone who can sit down," Mrs. Wilson said, smiling at the enormous egg, who could not fit on a chair in his costume. "I am handing out a slip of paper to each of you. After the reports are finished, we will vote for the best one."

When she reached Leo's seat, Mrs. Wilson frowned. "Leo, you were supposed to put your costume on in the classroom."

"My costume isn't something you can wear," Leo said. He lifted up the boxes from Dee Dee's so she would see that he wasn't empty-handed.

Mrs. Wilson did not look convinced. "I hope you've done the assignment."

"I have, Mrs. Wilson. Honest."

"Well, we'll soon see," she said, and passed on down the row.

Tommy Ryan gave the first report. It was about a boy in Colonial times who was apprenticed to Paul Revere. It sounded like an exciting book, but poor Tommy was all dressed up in knickers and a frilly shirt. He even had a three-cornered hat like the kind they sold at the historical museum, and fake metal buckles stuck onto his shoes. Tommy raced through his report as quickly as he could.

"His mother made him dress like that," Harry Nash whispered to Leo.

Next a girl came as Harriet the Spy, with her notebook, glasses, and hooded sweatshirt. Then the enormous egg waddled onstage to loud applause. Being the egg was easier than being the dinosaur that hatches from it, Leo thought to himself. The other benefit of being an egg was that no one could see you inside the costume.

Emily Mott was next in line. Leo watched with interest. What is she? he wondered, looking at her costume.

Emily was covered with string. It was all tied together in a crisscross pattern and attached to her shoulders, arms, hands, knees, and feet. Maybe she's a fish caught in a net, thought Leo. I bet her book is *The Fisherman and His Wife*.

When Emily reached the center of the stage, she stood with her legs wide apart and stretched her arms out to each side. Suddenly everyone in

the class gasped and laughed and clapped. The string across the front of Emily's costume was tied in such a way that it spelled *Some Pig.* Emily had come as Charlotte's web!

"Hey, Mott, how'd you do that?" Johnny Ringer called out from the back row.

Emily smiled and reached up to straighten her glasses. "I just tied lots of knots," she said. She seemed half proud and half embarrassed at all the attention. Leo liked her more than ever for not showing off. She never bragged about being smart.

"Excellent, Emily," said Mrs. Wilson. "Very imaginative."

The boy wearing his father's tuxedo jacket was supposed to be one of Mr. Popper's penguins. The tails of the coat dragged on the floor. The girl with the pinafore on was Laura in the "Little House" books. Ivy got a round of applause as Pippi Longstocking. Her braids stuck straight out, and one knee sock was up and the other was down. Everyone knew who she was right away.

Finally it was Leo's turn. He walked slowly up the steps and onto the stage carrying his book and the two boxes from Dee Dee's. No one laughed. Everyone sat quietly, watching.

First Leo stood the book up on the table in the center of the stage, so everyone could see the cover. Then he opened the boxes of doughnuts. All around the book he stacked the doughnuts, making towers of different heights. He made a tall tower of powdered doughnuts, one of glazed, and several mixed piles, using the chocolate doughnuts too. Homer Price's doughnuts were all plain, but Leo thought the variety would look better.

As the children saw all the doughnuts pile up on the table, they ohhed and ahhed. Will licked his lips and Ivy rubbed her stomach with her hand. Even Mrs. Wilson did not look so stern.

"My name is Homer Price," Leo began. He told a little about Homer's adventures, and he told the story of the doughnut machine from beginning to end. When he finished, he said, "And the only way to get rid of the rest of these doughnuts is for everyone to eat one."

With that, everyone in the class clapped. Leo went from seat to seat, giving out doughnuts.

There was even one for Mrs. Wilson, who nodded as if to say "Good job."

At the end of the book report presentations, the class voted. Mrs. Wilson collected the slips of paper and quickly sorted them out into piles and counted them.

"Boys and girls, the prize for the best costume goes to Richard Wittaker for his enormous egg."

Everyone clapped. Richard waddled to the stage again for his prize. It looked, of course, like a book. But Richard couldn't take it from Mrs. Wilson because his arms were trapped inside his giant shell.

"You may pick it up later, when you have taken off your costume," said the teacher.

"Yeah, when you get hatched," called out Johnny Ringer. Everyone laughed.

"The second prize goes to Emily Mott for her web."

The class clapped again. Her prize was also shaped like a book.

"And the third prize goes to Leo Nolan for his clever idea. Very original, Leo."

Leo was startled. His ears burned as the class clapped, and he knew they were turning red. He had to walk to the stage again with everyone watching. Mrs. Wilson handed him a package wrapped in green foil paper.

He said "Thank you," and gave the class an embarrassed smile as he walked back to his seat.

After school was dismissed for the day, Leo walked home slowly. He hadn't opened his prize yet. He was waiting to do that at home. It was a book, he knew. I hope it's funny, he thought. He remembered how surprised he had been when Mrs. Wilson had called out his name. He remembered his ears getting hot. But it was a nice memory. Nobody had laughed this time. Not once. They hadn't laughed, they'd clapped.

Leo stuck his hands in his pockets again and tried to walk like Homer Price, leaning back into the wind a little. He wasn't a clown any-more. He wasn't silly. He was clever, and origi-nal. Maybe next time he wouldn't even be embarrassed.

THE LIZARD LETDOWN

On his way home from school Leo often stopped to look in the pet store window. Sometimes there were puppies tumbling over each other or curled up in balls, sleeping. Sometimes there were kittens—striped ones and spotted ones—so little, they looked as if they had just opened their eyes. At Eastertime the window was filled with fat white rabbits. And once there was a parrot who sat on a stand and screamed, "Hello, Mac."

When he stopped to look on Wednesday, the window was filled with guinea pigs: a round brown one, a sleek black one, an orange one, a fluffy white one, and a little one with patches of every color, mixed up like a crazy quilt. The patchwork pig had an orange spot covering one eye and a brown spot circling the other. His back was a mixture of white, brown, black, and orange. Two feet were black, one was orange, and the other white. Leo laughed when he saw him. When the patchwork pig noticed Leo standing at the window with his nose pressed up against the glass, he began to make noise. "Wink, wink, wink-wink-wink," he said. His nose twitched like a rabbit and his round black eyes shone.

"Wink, wink, wink," Leo said in return. Then he looked around quickly to make sure no one was passing nearby. The sidewalk was empty. "Wink, wink," Leo bleated some more. The guinea pig answered back.

Leo stepped back from the glass to read the signs on the window.

GUINEA PIGS/ $6.00 each
CHAMELEONS / $3.75 each

Six dollars is a lot, Leo thought. Much more

than I've got. Maybe a chameleon would be better.

Leo had read about chameleons. They could change colors to match whatever you put them on. Only $3.75. I'd like a chameleon, he thought. I could carry him around and put him on top of different things and watch him change colors. Only $3.75.

Leo put his hand into his pocket and pulled out his change. Only thirty-five cents, and he had been planning to buy a chocolate crunch bar at the drugstore. There was no money left in his bank either.

He started home with his hands in his pockets, looking carefully at the sidewalk in hopes of finding some change. He picked up a penny in front of the barber shop and a nickel by the fire station. He checked every parking meter on Main Street, but there were no stuck coins. He checked the pay phones on the corner, but no one had forgotten any change. When he turned down his own block, after skipping the chocolate bar, he had forty-one cents in his pocket.

Not enough, thought Leo.

He was still thinking of the chameleon when

he reached his own yard. I bet that lizard could turn red and yellow just like all these leaves, he thought. Leaves! Leo looked down at the sidewalk. It was covered with leaves. So was the yard. And the yard next door at Mrs. Rider's house. I'll rake up the leaves and earn enough to buy that little lizard, Leo decided.

He dropped his knapsack on the back porch and found the rake in a corner of the garage. Mrs. Rider was likely to pay more than his parents, who would probably tell him that his allowance was payment enough. He went next door and rang Mrs. Rider's bell.

"Hello, Leo," said Mrs. Rider, taking her reading glasses off her nose.

"Want me to rake for you, Mrs. Rider?"

The old lady looked out at her yard. "Those leaves have fallen down in earnest, haven't they now? It must have been the rain last night. I don't remember there being so many before."

She scrutinized Leo with a frown. "You want to rake for me, do you?" She paused. "Well, Leo, I don't know. Do you remember what happened last year?"

Leo blushed and scratched the back of his knee with his foot. Last year he had agreed to rake for Mrs. Rider. He had raked all the leaves into a gigantic pile in the middle of the front yard. But before he could stuff the leaves into the big green plastic garbage bags, Bulldog Nelson, Tony Rosa, and two other older boys had come along.

"Hey, let's jump in those leaves," Bulldog yelled to the others.

"Wait. Wait a minute." Leo tried to stop them. But Tony just pushed him out of the way. "Step aside, short stuff," he said.

The four big boys jumped in the leaf pile again and again until the leaves were scattered all over the yard. Hearing their loud hoots and yells, Mrs. Rider came out of her house. She hated to have children playing in her front yard. "They'll ruin my azaleas," she always said.

"Get away from here, you boys. Get away. Right now," she said, walking stiffly down the front path, leaning on her cane. She stopped and pointed the cane at Leo.

"And you, young man. What have you got to say for yourself? Letting those hoodlums run all over this yard. You've done more harm than good."

Leo tried to explain, but he tripped over his words and felt foolish. He didn't want to admit that he was afraid of Bulldog and his friends. So he apologized, raked up the leaves again, and went home without collecting any pay.

"But that was last year, Mrs. Rider. I'm older now. You can trust me. Those big guys can't push me around now." Then an idea popped into Leo's mind. "Besides, this time I'll rake all the leaves into the backyard and nobody will be able to see the pile from the street."

Mrs. Rider peered at him closely once more. Then she smiled, and her stern expression thawed. "Very well, Leo. You may have a second chance. Let's say two dollars for the front and back yards, and another dollar if you'll bring in a supply of firewood from the garage and pile it neatly by the wood stove in the den. I like to keep warm when I read."

Leo quickly agreed. Three dollars. That made $3.41. With this week's allowance he'd have enough to buy that chameleon on Saturday.

He raked all the leaves into a pile in the backyard. They were wet and slippery from last night's rain, so he wasn't even tempted to jump into the pile himself. When he bundled the leaves together, they filled six garbage bags. Leo lugged them one at a time to the side of the house where the garbage cans stood.

The wood was heavy too. Leo made at least ten trips from the garage, piling the wood neatly by the wall in the bright yellow den. Mrs. Rider's wing chair stood between the window and the stove. Bookcases filled the opposite wall. It was a cheerful, sunny room, and the wood stove made it cozy. No wonder she likes to read in here, he thought.

Mrs. Rider offered Leo a glass of cold cider when he was finished. "Good work," she said as she gave him three dollar bills. Leo thanked her, put the money in his pocket, and headed home.

Only three days until he could buy the chameleon, he thought as he lay in bed that night. Tomorrow he would build a cage. There was leftover screening and wood in the basement. It wouldn't be hard. He would put in a branch for the lizard to climb on and a bed of moss for a soft place to lie. His paint dishes would be good for food and water.

I wonder what a lizard eats, he thought before he fell asleep.

He finished the cage on Thursday afternoon. His sister, Eleanor, got a look at it as Leo carried it up to his room.

"What's that?" she asked.

"A cage."

"I can see that, dopey. What's it for?"

Leo hesitated. He hadn't asked his parents about the lizard. If Eleanor made a fuss, maybe they wouldn't let him buy one.

"It's a cage for an animal."

"I figured *that*. It's too small for you."

Leo knew he couldn't stall any longer. Eleanor was getting irritated.

"It's for the new pet I'm buying on Saturday."

Eleanor eyed the construction. It didn't look very sturdy.

"It's escape-proof," Leo added.

"I've heard that one before. Like the time you brought your class mouse home."

It had taken Leo three weeks to find the mouse after it got loose.

"What kind of nasty little beast are you bringing home this time?"

Leo had to tell her. "It's a chameleon."

"Ugh! One of those creepy lizards? Why do you want to waste your money on something disgusting like that?"

"It's neat," protested Leo. "It turns colors. It won't bother you at all. I promise. So don't make a big deal out of this, okay?"

"You mean, with Mom and Dad?" Eleanor hesitated for a second, calculating her advantage. "I'll help you out if you promise not to tell that I've been keeping my light on late every night."

Leo had seen the light in Eleanor's room when he got up to go to the bathroom at night. He knew she was staying up, reading.

He agreed happily, thinking he had gotten the best of the bargain.

His parents did not protest too much.

"Are you sure that this is what you want?" his mother asked.

Leo was sure he was sure.

On Friday he spent the afternoon finding different-colored things to test his chameleon on. He made a pile on his bed.

First there was his red plaid bathrobe. It was a deep red, with lines of green, yellow, and white in it. The chameleon would look like a Scotch lizard when he landed on the bathrobe, Leo thought.

Next he borrowed the pink blotter from Eleanor's desk. She never used it anyway. It had come in a set that Grandma had sent, a pink desk set that said JUNIOR MISS on it in gold letters. Eleanor hated it.

Then he thought of his blue-and-yellow-striped tie, the one he had to wear for Christmas dinner and visits to his grandmother's. At least it will be good for something fun for a change, Leo thought.

In Leo's imagination his chameleon could turn every color of the rainbow.

On Saturday morning Leo collected his allowance from his father and headed downtown. The sign was still up in the pet shop window. The guinea pigs were still there too. At least three were—the shiny black one, the orange one, and the patchwork one.

Leo didn't stop to say "Wink, wink," this time. He rushed right inside. The chameleons were crawling around in a tank on the counter.

"One chameleon, please," Leo said to the pet store owner.

"Three seventy-five," said the man, assembling a little square white box with a wire handle.

Leo counted out his money and put it on the counter. The man reached inside the tank.

"Is there one in particular that you want?"

They all looked alike. But one blinked his eyes twice and Leo decided that he must be signaling him.

"That one," he said, pointing to the lizard that had blinked.

The pet store man picked up the chameleon and put him in the box. It looked like a container of Chinese food. Boy, wouldn't somebody be surprised if he opened this up expecting egg foo yung, Leo thought.

"Do you know how to take care of this lizard?" asked the man.

Leo shook his head.

"Fresh water, lettuce, and mealy worms. You can grow them yourself. Here are the instructions and a bunch to start with."

They were disgusting! Little white worms

crawling in a heap. Ugh! Who ever thought chameleons would eat anything so awful-looking.

"You put these worms on some oatmeal and they'll start reproducing. You'll have a colony in no time," said the man cheerfully.

And my mother will have a fit, Leo thought.

He took the bag with the lizard, the worms, and a care-and-feeding sheet and thanked the man. Then he stopped by the window on his way out. The patchwork pig seemed to recognize him right away.

"Wink. Wink-wink," he bleated, and raced around in a circle.

"Wink-wink, yourself," Leo answered. "I bet you don't eat worms."

He put the bag in his bike basket and headed home.

Up in his room Leo set the chameleon container on his desk and opened the top of the cage. Then he lifted the flaps of the white box. The lizard was moving around in the bottom, trying to climb the sides. His claws rasped against the cardboard. Leo tentatively reached a finger into the box to feel the lizard's skin. It was cool, dry, and bumpy; not slimy but still a little creepy. The lizard squirmed away, not enjoying the encounter any more than Leo.

Leo decided not to pick the chameleon up just yet. Instead, he upended the box and slid the surprised lizard into his new home. He landed on the moss but quickly scampered up the branch and perched there quivering, his eyes darting around the cage.

Leo dumped a blob of worms into the food dish and watched his chameleon for a while. But the lizard did not move, and finally, feeling slightly disappointed, Leo went down to lunch.

"Wash your hands well if you've been touching that animal," said Leo's mother as she put Leo's sandwich in front of him.

"I only touched him with one finger," Leo said.

"That's enough. Wash up."

Leo decided not to mention the mealy worms during lunch. It was probably not table talk, as his mother always said.

After lunch he went back upstairs. The chameleon had not moved. Maybe it wouldn't be so hard to pick him up after all.

Leo spread his bathrobe on the bed. Next to it he placed the pink blotter. Then, finally, he draped his tie across the bedspread.

"Time to experiment," he announced. "Introducing the rainbow lizard."

The chameleon sat on the branch in his cage, so still that he didn't seem alive. Leo carefully opened the top and reached in. Just as his hand came down on the chameleon, it whisked away to the other side of the cage.

"Oh-ho! Tricky, eh?" Leo reached again and missed.

He finally cornered the lizard between the screen and the branch and picked him up. The chameleon wiggled madly for a second and then was very still. Quick, abrupt moves were his specialty. Leo kept his hand firmly around him even though he didn't like the way he felt.

"Time to see what you can do."

He placed the chameleon on top of the red-plaid bathrobe, making a fence around him with his legs. The lizard sat there, blinking. He turned his head so one beady little eye was staring straight at Leo. Leo watched and waited. The chameleon was brown. The bathrobe was a bright red plaid. Leo waited and watched carefully to see the transformation.

Nothing happened.

The chameleon remained brown. He didn't turn even the slightest bit red.

Maybe plaid is too hard to start with, Leo thought, beginning to feel worried about his investment. He probably has to start off on something easier. Leo pushed the lizard farther over until he was standing on the pink blotting paper and watched carefully. The lizard stuck out his tongue, but it was red, not pink. His skin stayed brown. He was definitely not cooperating with the experiment.

After waiting for a few minutes, Leo decided to try the tie.

"Maybe these bright colors are too difficult for you," he said to the chameleon, moving him over onto the tie. "If you can't do the stripe, at least try to turn blue."

The chameleon remained a dull brown.

"What a gyp! What good are you, anyway?"

He picked up the little lizard and put him back in the cage, setting him down on the moss. This time the chameleon stayed there instead of climbing the branch. Gradually he turned from a dull brown to a dull green.

Leo watched the change. "Okay. At least you can do something. Brown and green. Is that all?" He was very disappointed. "I wonder if those are the only colors you turn." Maybe the rainbow lizard existed only in his imagination.

There was a set of encyclopedias in Eleanor's room. Leo found what he was hunting for in volume three. It even had a little drawing that looked exactly like his lizard. The description said that they only turn colors for camouflage, and can become green or brown depending on their surroundings.

"What a gyp," Leo repeated. "Three dollars and seventy-five cents, and he doesn't know any good colors. And I have to grow his disgusting old worms."

He went back into his room to look at his pet. There wasn't really anything he could do with the lizard. He wasn't any fun to play with. He didn't make any noises. He wasn't even good to pet.

The white box was still standing next to the cage. In a flash Leo decided what to do. He trapped the lizard again and lifted him out. Then he dumped him back into the container and folded down the top. He looked at the clock. Three forty-five. Plenty of time to get downtown.

The pet store was still open when Leo pulled up on his bike. And the patchwork pig was still in the window. Leo crossed his toes inside his sneakers for luck as he waited at the counter.

"Back already?" said the pet store man when it was Leo's turn.

Leo put the chameleon container on the counter. "Do you think I could trade this lizard in?"

"Trade it in for what?"

Leo glanced back at the window. "For the guinea pig with all the different colors. I know I need another two twenty-five, but I'll earn that by Monday. Could you take this lizard back and keep my three seventy-five as a down payment on a guinea pig?"

Leo held his breath as he waited for the answer.

The man opened the box and looked at the chameleon. "Looks none the worse for wear," he said.

He dumped the chameleon back into the cage with the others. It darted around until it found a space behind a piece of bark.

"Which guinea pig did you say?"

"The spotted one with all the different colors."

"Oh. The patchwork pig. All right, I'll hold it for you."

Before he left, Leo reached in and gave the patchwork pig a pat. His fur was soft and his nose was cold. His whiskers tickled as he sniffed Leo's hand.

"I'll call you Patches."

Leo spent Sunday raking leaves in three other yards. By dinnertime his arms ached, but he had made five dollars. Enough for the guinea pig, a book on how to care for him, and the water bottle that he needed for drinking.

He went by after school on Monday to pick him up. The man put the guinea pig in a large white box with air holes. Leo carried him home carefully. The pig did not make a sound the whole trip. Not a single "wink."

"Don't be scared," Leo said in a soft voice.

Up in his room Leo set the box softly on his

bed. Then he emptied out all of the moss and branches from the cage. He lined the bottom with a thick layer of newspaper and bunched soft pieces of towel in the corner.

"That's for your bed," he said to the guinea pig, who was still in the box.

Next Leo fastened the water bottle to the side of the cage. "All set," he said as he opened the box.

The guinea pig looked up with his shiny round eyes. His nose twitched. Leo gave his soft fur a pat with his finger. Then he reached underneath and picked him up. The guinea pig was surprisingly heavy. Leo could feel his heart beating against his side.

"Hey, don't be scared," he said again.

He set the guinea pig down gently in his new home. The animal waddled around the edges of the cage sniffing the corners. He licked the spout of the water bottle. Then he lay down on the towel.

Leo watched him closely, anxious to make sure he was comfortable. "Welcome home, Patches," he said. "I bet you're hungry."

He raced downstairs and scrounged in the

refrigerator vegetable bin. He found two carrots that were starting to shrivel and started back upstairs. When he reached the top step, Patches began to make noise.

"Wink, wink. Wink-wink," he bleated when he heard Leo coming.

"Hold on, Patches. I'm on my way," Leo called. He grinned as he skipped down the hall, a carrot in each hand. I bet he'll call me like this every day when I get home from school, Leo thought. A pet who says hello, now that's something special.

LEO'S WiLD iMAGiNATiON

Zing

Zat

"Children, line up in alphabetical order, please—boys by the bulletin board and girls over by the windows," Mrs. Wilson said. She stood at the front of the room holding the blue spelling book.

Leo got up very slowly. He stacked his books carefully in his desk and even put his pencil in his pencil case. He didn't really care about having a neat desk; he just wanted to postpone the spelling bee as long as possible. He had known it was coming. Mrs. Wilson had given out the assignment last week so they could study.

"Get on line, Leo. It's time to start." Mrs. Wilson eyed him sternly. She knew he was stalling.

Leo found his place between Harry and Ed. They were the three N's—Nash, Nolan, and Nye. Harry was an even worse speller than Leo.

Ivy Adams was the first one up. Her word was *able,* and she spelled it correctly. Leo frowned. He would have spelled it a-b-e-l. Usually Mrs. Wilson started with the easy words. If that was so easy, what would the hard words be like?

Ivy moved to the end of the girls' line, giving Leo an encouraging wink as she passed. She knew he hated spelling.

Leo hated a lot of things about school. He hated having to get up in front of the class, even though he had managed to do well on Book

Report Day. He didn't like reading out loud either. It made him feel silly and self-conscious. Some mornings he walked to school as slowly as possible, and all day long he couldn't wait to get outside again; and some days he seemed always to be in trouble, even though he tried to do things right.

Last year Leo had been a class clown. Loud Leo, the kids had called him. But he got tired of being a clown, and this year he was trying hard to be just Leo. Not Loud Leo. Not Leo the clown. Just Leo. He didn't want to be the smartest, or the dumbest. He just wanted to blend in. And some days he managed. Some days, like Book Report Day, he even felt proud and happy. But usually he just wanted the day to slip by as smoothly and quickly as possible. Then he could race down the steps, take a gulp of fresh air, and have the afternoon to himself.

Leo gave Ivy a half smile and tried to pay attention. The next word was *about*. Thomas Avery left out the *u* and had to sit down and study his speller. Leo let out a deep breath. It was always worse to be the first one out. At least now it wouldn't be him. Thomas shrugged and sauntered down the row to his seat, trying to look pleased to be out of the contest.

"A-l-l-i-g-a-t-o-r." Freddie Duncan spelled it right. The word reminded Leo of a movie he had seen at the Saturday matinee last month. He thought about alligators swimming in a jungle river, snapping their jaws. He was paddling along in his canoe, a long sleek boat. He was searching for treasure, a hoard of gold and precious jewels hidden somewhere in the jungle.

He paddled along, silently dipping his oar into the murky water. Huge alligators slithered off the banks and came sliding through the water. Their mean little eyes glowed above the dark river. The largest one opened his jaws and—

Leo jumped as Ed jabbed him in the ribs.

"Move up!"

The line had moved ahead at least three people while Leo was daydreaming.

When it was Leo's turn, Mrs. Wilson said the word slowly. "Astronaut." Leo's stomach uncoiled. It was a word that he knew. He liked to

read about space exploration. He spelled it carefully in three parts: "A-s, t-r-o, n-a-u-t."

Mrs. Wilson smiled and nodded. Leo went to the back of the line, feeling temporarily relieved. He jabbed Harry lightly in the arm and flipped his eyebrows up and down twice.

The line kept moving forward. Leo looked at the clock. One thirty-five. Six children were sitting down now, four boys and two girls. That left seventeen children still on line. Sam Brennon was absent. Boy, is he lucky to miss this, Leo thought.

The words were in the C's now: *carriage, caterpillar, certain, chocolate.* Leo tried to put them all together.

Are you certain that the caterpillar in the carriage is eating chocolate?

He imagined a big fat caterpillar riding in a shiny yellow baby carriage, chomping on a chocolate bar.

Ed poked him again. It was Leo's turn. He looked around quickly. Three more people had dropped out, including Harry.

Leo stepped up. Mrs. Wilson said the word clearly: "Circus." Leo thought of a big striped tent with a ring filled with sawdust. He could spell *clown* and even *elephant*. He could spell *sideshow* and *tiger* and *monkey*. He could even spell *acrobat*. He took a deep breath and started.

"C (pause). I (pause). R (pause). At least he knew the beginning. He took another breath, looked sideways at Mrs. Wilson, and raced through the next three letters in a hurry, hoping he'd get them right: "C-i-s."

One of the girls snickered. Leo couldn't tell who.

"No, Leo, that is incorrect. Take a seat and study your book," Mrs. Wilson said.

Emily Mott was next. She spelled it quickly in a soft voice. "C-i-r-c-u-s." As she walked to the back of the line she gave Leo a quick smile. He could tell that she wished he had gotten it right. But he didn't mind. At least he wasn't the first one out.

Sitting at his desk, Leo floated back into his jungle daydream, paddling bravely through the dark water, avoiding the alligators' jaws. On the banks of the river stood huge trees covered with vines. Monkeys swung from tree to tree. Red-and-green parrots screeched. It was hot.

Leo searched the jungle for the clue, crossed arrows carved in the trunk of a baobab tree. He shielded his eyes with his hand as he peered into the jungle.

"Yes. Leo? What is it?"

Mrs. Wilson's voice made him jump. He looked up in dazed confusion. His jungle was gone.

Mrs. Wilson frowned from the front of the room. "You raised your hand, Leo. What do you want? Do you need to be excused?"

Leo nodded, grateful that she had given him an excuse. He must have put his hand up when he was shielding his eyes.

Drat those daydreams! Always getting me into trouble.

With his ears burning, Leo left the room to get a drink of water. I have too much imagination, he thought. That's the problem.

The rest of the week Leo tried very hard to pay attention in school. It wasn't until Friday that his imagination got the best of him again. The art teacher, Mrs. Van Slyke, came to class on Friday. She handed out large pieces of drawing paper, so big that they covered a desk.

"Now, children, the assignment today is to draw your own house, giving as much detail as you can possibly fit in. Make these drawings very realistic. Now come up and select your drawing materials and then get started. At the end of the class we will put the drawings up on the wall and discuss them."

Mrs. Van Slyke set out boxes of crayons, cans filled with skinny markers, and tins of charcoal and pastels. Leo decided to work with markers. He picked out red, orange, brown, green, and gray. I'll do the sky later, he decided.

First Leo drew the shape of his house. It was two stories high. He added the door and the windows, and put the chimney on top, with the TV antenna perched up high.

"Give as much detail as you can remember. There's lots of room on those pieces of paper."

Leo added the tree by the side of the house, with the rope swing he had made with his dad last summer. The swing always hung kind of crooked. They hadn't measured the ropes right. So Leo drew it crooked, just the way it was.

"Use your memories, boys and girls."

Leo drew the bushes in front of the porch.

One time he had tried to jump from the railing clear over the bushes, onto the grass. But he hadn't jumped far enough. He had landed right in the middle of the bushes. The hole was still there. Leo left a space in the bushes for the hole.

The picture still looked bare. He drew in the shutters and colored the roof. The sky was blank. He went up to the front of the room and picked out a blue marker. Back at his seat he drew the outline of clouds, intending to leave them white. One cloud looked like a floppy pizza, one looked like a cowboy hat, and one looked like a flying saucer.

Leo stared at the flying saucer, trying to imagine what kind of creatures were inside. There's only one way to find out, he thought, and that's make them land and get out.

He drew the saucer coming down from the sky, using lots of arrows to show that it was moving. It was trying to land.

Wait! It wasn't so easy. There were fighter planes shooting at the saucer. Leo drew them in, using the dark gray marker. The planes were fast. Bullets crisscrossed the sky above the house. Leo softly made the sound effects as he drew.

"Zing. Zap. Rat-a-tat-a-tat. Piong. Zat. Splat. Rat-a-tat-a-tat," he whispered to himself.

Despite the bullets, the saucer managed to land right on the roof. The invaders climbed out. They were little green men. Using the green marker, Leo lined them up on the roof. One green man tried to climb in the chimney. Another began to slide down the drainpipe. He landed by the rosebushes and began to climb in the dining-room window.

"Time is up, class. Please sign your pictures and bring them to the front of the room."

Leo looked up with a start. He had forgotten all about the assignment. All he was thinking about was the flying saucer and its inhabitants.

He looked down at his paper. Oh, no! It was all there in bright colors: the saucer, the green men, the fighter planes, even the bullets. Oh, well, what could he do now? He signed his name, using the tiniest letters he could write, and carried his picture up to the front of the room.

Mrs. Van Slyke attached it to the board with

masking tape. She hung it right next to a picture of an apartment building complete with fire escape and parking lot. She put on her glasses and peered closely at Leo's picture.

"Now, what are these green things on the roof, Leo? Is that some sort of vine, or is it the top of a tree in your backyard? I can't make it out."

Leo's classmates all looked at his picture too. A few of the boys up front saw what it was right away.

"Martians on the roof!"

"Is that the ship, Nolan? That funny-shaped cloud?"

Leo nodded, half proud and half worried. He kept his eyes on Mrs. Van Slyke. She continued to stare at the board. A deep frown creased between her eyebrows.

"Leo, did you understand the assignment?"

Leo nodded, his head drooping.

"Well, then, why isn't this picture realistic? I asked for realistic detail, not imaginative foolishness! You'll have to do this assignment over again this weekend."

She pulled the offending picture off the board

and handed it to Leo. He rolled it up, sighing as he stuffed it into his knapsack. He hadn't meant to do it wrong. It just got away from him, that's all. Imagination! It would be easier not to have any.

After the dismissal bell rang, Leo was heading down the steps when Will and Charley Johnson raced up beside him.

"Hey, Leo, hold on. We want to see your house picture again."

Leo stopped walking. "You mean, the one I did in class?"

Will nodded. "Yes, the one with the guys landing on the roof. What a great idea! You have a wild imagination, Leo!"

Leo unrolled the picture and spread it out on the playground.

"Look at those fighter planes."

"I like the way you made the saucer land on the roof."

Leo nodded and smiled tentatively.

"Hey, Charley, look at this guy. He's breaking in through the window." Will pointed to the green man who had slid down the drainpipe.

Leo rolled up the picture again and put it back in his knapsack.

Charley pounded him on the shoulder. "You know what? I'm going home and fix up my picture. I'm going to add a monster. He'll be coming out of the ground maybe."

Leo walked home beside his friends, half listening to their plans. He felt a little better, but he was still upset about getting into trouble.

He was still worried about it after dinner.

"Want to do a puzzle with me?" his dad asked after Mrs. Nolan and Eleanor had left for the movies.

"Sure. Which one?"

"I brought home a new one. It's over on the game shelf."

Leo found the new puzzle on top of the pile of games. It had giant gumdrops all over it. He dumped it out on the table by the fireplace and began to turn over the pieces.

"How about some popcorn and a fire?" asked his father, rumpling Leo's hair.

Leo just nodded. He didn't even smile.

Mr. Nolan eyed him closely, then began to build the fire. When it was burning steadily, he went into the kitchen to make the popcorn. Leo could hear him singing as he shook the kernels back and forth in the saucepan. In a few minutes Mr. Nolan returned carrying a tray with two bowls of popcorn, a glass of ginger ale, and a bottle of beer. "All set."

Leo said "Thanks," and kept on trying to fit the border pieces together. Mr. Nolan joined him. For a while they worked in silence. The only sound was the crackling of the fire. Leo let out a long sigh.

Mr. Nolan looked up. "You seem preoccupied, Leo. Maybe even a little sad. What's up?"

Leo hesitated a second before answering.

"Do you think it's possible to have too much imagination?"

"What do you mean?"

"Imagination. You know, getting crazy ideas. Daydreams."

"Do you think you have too much?"

Leo nodded glumly. "I know it!"

"What happened?"

Leo told his father all about the spelling bee, and the art lesson. Mr. Nolan listened carefully. Several times his mouth turned up at the corners and it looked as if he would laugh, but he took a sip of beer instead.

Leo finished his story with a shake of his head. "That's why I think I have too much imagination." He reached for a handful of popcorn.

His father sat and thought for a minute. Then he answered slowly. "I don't think it's possible to have too much imagination. I think the world needs just as much imagination as we can give it."

Leo looked unconvinced.

His father continued. "Imagination is what solves problems. Inventors have it, and scientists. There'd be no space travel if it wasn't for imagination. There'd be no stories or pictures or music."

"But, Dad—"

"I know, you think imagination got you into trouble, but I don't think so. It wasn't your imagination that got you into trouble, it was your concentration. You can't keep your mind on what you're doing, right?"

Leo agreed.

"Well, cheer up. That's something you can practice. I know. I used to be a terrible daydreamer."

"You were?"

"You bet I was! One time in high school math class, I was thinking about my girlfriend instead of the geometry problem, and instead of saying 'parallel,' I said 'Pamela.' Everyone laughed. I turned bright red, I was so embarrassed. That's when I vowed I'd get it under control."

"And did you?"

"I sure did. I picked out the times when it was okay to let my mind run loose. Like walking to school, or sitting in study hall, or lying in bed. I really enjoyed daydreaming!" Mr. Nolan leaned across the table. "Want to know the best place to daydream? When you're soaking in the bathtub."

Leo shook his head. "Not for me. I like showers."

"Okay, then. You'll have to think of your own times. And practice keeping your focus at school." Mr. Nolan took another swallow of beer. "You know what I think, Leo? I think you're very lucky to have that imagination. You make life more interesting."

Leo frowned. He didn't understand.

"Take that spelling bee. Was that very interesting?"

"NO!"

"But your daydream was, right? And the art

assignment that you made up was much more interesting than the one Mrs. What's-her-name gave you, right? Your friends certainly thought so."

Leo thought about it for a minute while he searched for a puzzle piece with a little red and a lot of yellow.

"I guess you're right," he admitted.

"Sure, I'm right!" Mr. Nolan looked very pleased with himself. "Imagination is a talent! Daydreaming is an art! You just need to figure out when to do it and when not to do it."

The fire was almost burned down, and they had finished only half the puzzle, when Mr. Nolan looked at his watch and said, "Time for bed."

Leo went up without a protest. After his father had kissed him good night, he lay on his back with his arms crossed behind his head.

It felt good to lie in bed and stare at the darkness. He let his mind wander, waiting for his imagination to turn up some exciting thoughts. But before he could begin to daydream, his eyes grew heavy and he fell asleep. He started his night dreams instead.

THE LOST DOG

"Atta-boy, Leo, go for it," Will called as Leo caught the football and started down the field. He dodged Jimmy Evans and outran the boy from Maple Street. The field was muddy from several days of fall rain. Leo's feet squished in the wet grass, sending up sprays of brown water as he ran. The only one behind him now was Charley Johnson, and he was a fast runner. Leo zigzagged to the left and then to the right again, trying to throw Charley off his track. Only a few more yards to a touchdown.

Charley dove for Leo's feet, but Leo jumped out of the way and reached the end line in three long strides. But just as he crossed the line his foot slipped on the mud and down he fell. Splat! Flat on his back.

"Touchdown!" his teammates yelled.

Leo lay on his back clutching the football, trying to catch his breath. He was staring up at the gray, cloudy sky when a black-and-white muzzle blocked his view and a warm pink tongue licked his face.

"Hey! What's going on?" Leo sat up quickly and found himself face-to-face with a dalmatian. The dog's tail was wagging eagerly, and his head was cocked to one side.

"Woof, woof," barked the dog, pawing the ground as if to say "Get up and play with me."

Leo patted his head. "Good dog!"

The dog licked his hand and wagged his tail some more.

Leo stood up and scraped some of the mud off the seat of his jeans. The dog was doing an eager little dance around him, barking softly. He was a black-and-white dalmatian with long, coltish legs. He must still be a pup, Leo thought, watching his awkward jumps. He gave the dog another pat and headed back to the game. The puppy followed close on his heels, whining and barking short yelps.

"Shoo, boy. Off the field." Leo waved him out of the way. "No dogs allowed in the game."

The pup paid no attention, and Leo finally had to pull him by the scruff of his neck.

"Stay, boy. Sit. Right here. Now, STAY." Leo pushed the dog into a sitting position on the sideline. The dog whined and cocked his head to the side again, but made no move to get up.

"Good boy," Leo said, and returned to the game.

The game lasted fifteen minutes more before the cold November rain put an end to it. The boys scurried for shelter under the pines by the side of the field, pulling on their jackets. Leo was zipping up his hooded sweatshirt when he noticed the dalmatian sitting off to the side. His ears were perked in a quizzical expression, and his eyes were fixed on Leo. When Leo looked his way, the dog's tail wagged back and forth, splashing a puddle behind him.

"Whose dog is that?" Leo asked.

"Never saw him before," Charley answered.

"Me neither," said Will.

The others shook their heads. No one recognized the black-and-white pup.

"Here, pup," said Leo. The dog trotted over and licked his hand with his warm, rough tongue. It tickled.

"See you tomorrow, Leo," said Will, heading for home.

"Bye," said Leo, waving to his friends as they ran off in the darkening rain. In just a few minutes Leo was standing alone with the dog.

"Go home," Leo said.

The dog wagged his tail and stayed by Leo's side.

"What am I going to do with you now? I can't leave you out here in the rain. You better come with me."

When they reached Leo's house, both boy and dog were soaking wet.

"We better use the back door," Leo said to the dripping pup.

As they stood in the kitchen, the rain running off them gathered in puddles on the floor.

"Leo, what on earth?" his mother said. "You wait right here while I get a towel."

She brought down a towel for each of them. Leo dried himself off and then rubbed the dog dry. As he was rubbing, the puppy licked his face lovingly, his tail pounding on the kitchen floor.

"Hey, cut it out. You're getting me wet again," Leo said. But the dog kept right on kissing his face.

"Where did you find your furry friend?" Mrs. Nolan asked.

"He found me. Over in the park. Nobody knew who owns him. I couldn't leave him out in the rain. I told him to go home, but he stuck right by me." Leo looked up at his mother. His eyes pleaded with her, just as the puppy's eyes had pleaded with him. "Do you think I could keep him? Please, Mom?"

Mrs. Nolan patted the dog's head and scratched him behind his ears. "He seems like a nice dog, Leo. I wouldn't be surprised if he was purebred. A real dalmatian. If that's so, then he may be valuable. He must belong to somebody."

"But who, Mom?"

"I don't know, Leo. We'll put an ad in the paper and see if we can find his owner."

"Do we have to? Can't we just keep him?"

"No, honey. His owner may be searching for him right now."

Leo thought about the situation for a minute. He wished they didn't have to place the ad. "But, Mom, how will we know that the person who calls is really the owner?"

"We won't describe him. We'll just say 'lost dog,' and tell where and when you found him. Then the people who call will describe their dogs and we'll know if the dog they lost is this dog."

Mr. Nolan agreed when he came home that night, and he said he would place the ad the next day when he went to work.

"What if nobody calls?" Leo asked.

"Then the dog will be yours," said his father. "You'll have to take good care of him, just the way you take care of Patches."

Leo looked at the spotted puppy. "I'm going to call him Chief, like fire chief."

Chief wagged his tail. He wagged his tail whenever he heard Leo say anything.

"See. He likes his name. Don't you, Chief?"

The dog rested his head on Leo's knee and looked up at him with big dark eyes.

Mr. Nolan watched the two of them with a look of concern on his face. "Remember," he warned Leo. "This is probably someone else's dog. He may not be staying here very long. Don't get your hopes up. You may be disappointed."

Leo smoothed the hair between Chief's ears. He didn't pay much attention to what his father was saying.

That night, when Leo climbed into bed, Chief hopped up too. Leo tucked his feet up to make room. When his mother kissed Leo good night, Chief was curled up comfortably at the end of the bed.

"Sleep tight, you two," she said as she turned off the light.

Leo closed his eyes. He could hear Chief breathing deeply. From time to time Chief would let out a deep sigh, sounding very contented. Leo was almost asleep when Chief yawned, wiggled around, and changed positions, stretching out lengthwise. But the bed was too narrow, and Chief's feet hung off the side. So he made a half turn and lay alongside Leo with his head up near Leo's arm.

Leo moved over a little to make room for his guest. Chief sighed contentedly once more.

Leo closed his eyes and drifted off to sleep. It had been an exciting day. He was tired. He had only been asleep a short time when "Oof!" He woke with a jolt. Something was prodding him in the middle of his back. He looked over his shoulder.

Chief had unfolded his long legs, and in his sleep he was pushing Leo right off the bed!

"Chief! Move over!" Leo pried Chief's legs away from his back and shoved him over to the edge of the bed. Chief opened one eye and looked at Leo accusingly, as if to say "How could you disturb me so rudely?"

"This is *my* bed, remember?" Leo said, and settled on his side again, in the middle of the mattress.

When Leo woke up in the morning, Chief was lying with his head on the pillow, his cold wet nose resting right on Leo's neck.

"Chief, move over, you big bed-hog. Next thing I know, you'll be kissing me good morning!"

Chief's tail beat gently against the quilt. He looked at Leo with loving eyes, as if he would be happy to give him a kiss.

Just then Eleanor leaned in the doorway. "Time to get up, Leo." She noticed Chief. "Ugh! You let that smelly old dog sleep in your bed with his head on your pillow? Disgusting. Think of all those fleas. You better not tell Mom."

Leo jumped to his dog's defense. "He doesn't have fleas. No more than you've got in your head, anyway."

Eleanor ignored the insult. "Better hurry or you'll be late."

Chief had to stay home while Leo went to school, but he was waiting eagerly by the front door when Leo returned.

"Leo, get that dog out of the house this afternoon," his mother called when she heard the door open. "He's driving me mad. How can I get any work done with that crazy dog following me around wanting to play? That scamp has gotten into everything."

She showed Leo a chewed slipper, an overturned garbage pail, a scratched door, and a large wet spot on the living-room rug.

"And I have a Friday deadline for this article. Really, Leo, he is a nuisance. I hope somebody claims him soon."

Leo picked up the scattered garbage and scrubbed the rug. "We better get out of here," he said to Chief, who did not look the least bit contrite. They headed for the park and did not return until dinnertime.

The newspaper ad ran the next day, and that evening there were four calls for the lost dog. The first caller was a boy who had lost a brown mutt named Bones. The second call came from a lady whose white poodle had run away from the Poodle Palace Salon, where it was getting a shampoo. The third caller was a man who was looking for a collie. "He often wanders off for a few days," he said. "I'm sure he'll turn up soon." The fourth person to call was an old lady whose cocker spaniel was missing. "I'm afraid she's been run over. She can't move quickly anymore, and she doesn't hear the cars coming. Well, thank you very much. I'll just keep on looking." She sounded sad and lonely. Leo wished he had found her dog for her.

Each time the phone rang, Leo's heart beat

fast. He was sure the caller would ask for a dalmatian, and he would have to give Chief back.

Chief lay sprawled out on the living-room rug, not the least bit worried about the phone calls.

When it was time for bed, Leo begged to stay up longer. "But what if someone calls after I'm asleep and asks for Chief? I won't even know that I've lost him until morning."

"Don't worry. That probably won't happen. Most people call early in the evening. Chief will be here in the morning," Mr. Nolan reassured him.

Leo kissed his parents good night and went upstairs, with Chief following right behind him. He put on his pajamas and brushed his teeth. When he came back to his room, Chief had already stretched out comfortably in the middle of the bed, leaving hardly any room for Leo.

Leo looked at the dog and thought for a minute. "Fair is fair. We'll have a race from the end of the hall. First one to the bed gets the middle. The other one has to sleep on the side."

Chief's tail thumped against the bed even though he didn't understand what Leo was saying.

"Okay. This is how we do it," Leo explained. "You get down from there. And I'll turn down the covers. Then you come with me. We'll race from the top of the stairs."

Leo led the way down the hall. Chief followed trustingly. When they reached the top of the staircase, Leo turned and faced his room. Patches, the guinea pig, cheered from his cage. "Wink, wink," he squeaked.

"On the count of three we'll start."

Chief cocked his head to one side, not understanding the game. He liked to play, but he didn't know what Leo was up to.

"Okay. On your mark. Get set. GO!"

Leo raced down the hall. Chief caught on and ran after him. But Leo had a head start, and he reached the bed first, thrusting his legs under the covers. Chief jumped up beside him. He had lost his sleeping place. He whined and looked at Leo with his big dark eyes, as if to say "How could you trick me?"

"Well," said Leo, "it is my bed, you know."

Two people called the next night, but neither one asked for a dalmatian. Leo began to think that Chief was his for good. He took Chief with him everywhere—to the store, to the park, to the woods behind the railroad tracks. He tied him to a tree outside the library when he went in to find a book. And he tied him on the porch when he visited Will, whose mother was allergic to dogs. He played with Chief every afternoon, and went to sleep with Chief at his side each night. By the end of a week Leo was sure that the dog would be his forever.

"Mom, I think we should buy a big sack of dog food for Chief," Leo said.

"I'd wait a bit longer, Leo. A dalmatian like Chief is a special dog. His owner may still turn up," his mother cautioned.

But Leo wasn't worried. He knew Chief was staying for good.

The next afternoon Leo was playing football with his friends. Chief sat on the sidelines and watched. In the middle of the game Leo noticed a dark blue car driving very slowly around the edge of the park. The car circled the block twice, inching slowly along, as if the driver was looking very carefully at something.

I wonder what he wants, Leo thought. The

park was nothing special. It didn't even have swings or a climbing frame. Just a sandbox for the little kids and this big field for playing. Nothing special to look at. Just a bunch of guys playing football and a dog watching.

A dog!

Maybe he was looking for a dog.

Leo felt a chill slide down his back. The car was circling the block for the third time. What should I do? Leo wondered.

He looked over at Chief. Maybe I can sneak him back home. If I keep behind the trees, the man in the car might not see me. The guys will cover for me. They can say they never saw me before. They can tell him I live in some other part of town.

Leo shook his head. He didn't want to sneak and hide. And he didn't want his friends to have to lie for him either. He stayed on the field.

The blue car pulled over by the curb and a tall thin man stepped out. He was wearing a baggy sweater. His face was windburned and his eyes crinkled up at the corners. He smiled as he walked across the field.

Chief went running toward him, wagging his tail so hard that his whole rear end wiggled back and forth. "Woof, woof. Wer-roof, woo-oof." Chief barked and whined his greeting.

The man crouched down and gave Chief a big hug, rubbing his back and scratching his ears. Chief covered his face with licks, speaking in soft happy yelps.

Leo watched with his hands on his hips. He could not smile, even though Chief looked so delighted. He knew that this tall man had come to claim his dog, and he wished for all the world that he had stayed at home today, keeping Chief safely hidden.

The stranger looked up at the boys who had gathered together near Leo. "Who should I be thanking for finding Freckles?"

What a stupid name, Leo thought. He didn't want to answer the man's question.

"Leo found him," Will said, giving reluctant Leo a push forward.

Leo stared at his sneakers. He didn't want to look up and see his dog wagging his tail at somebody else.

"So you found this rascal, did you? I'm very

grateful to you, son. This dog means a lot to me. I've had him since he was born. His mother was my dog. Her name was Rosie."

Another stupid name, Leo thought, still staring at his sneakers.

"What's your name, son?"

"Leo Nolan."

"Freckles is in fine shape, Leo. I can tell he's been well cared for. Let me follow you home. I'd like to thank your parents and pay for Freckles's food. Where do you live?"

"In the third house from the corner. It's white with a porch."

The man got back in his car and drove down the street. Slowly Leo walked home with Chief. He tried very hard to hold back his tears. He didn't want to cry in front of the man.

At the Nolans' Leo's mother greeted Chief's owner, whose name was Mr. Edwards. They went into the living room and sat down. Mrs. Nolan kept her arm around Leo's shoulders. Mr. Nolan arrived home just as they were beginning to talk.

"Nice to meet you, Mr. Edwards," Leo's father said. "Can't say we're happy to see you. Leo's grown very fond of Chief."

"Freckles," Mr. Edwards corrected.

"Yes, of course, Freckles. As I was saying, the dog's been here over a week, and my son has taken excellent care of him."

"I can see that," Mr. Edwards interrupted. "Freckles looks well fed, and he's certainly attached to your boy. I'm grateful to you and I'd like to pay you back for the food." He reached for his wallet.

"Wait just a minute. I'm hoping you might consider this idea. Leo and Chief have been inseparable. Why not keep them together? Let me buy the dog from you."

Leo jumped to his feet, keeping his eyes on his father. Oh, thank you, Dad! Thanks! Leo said silently. He held his breath, waiting for the answer.

Mr. Edwards looked at Leo and then at the dog, who was lying in front of the fireplace. He shrugged his shoulders helplessly.

"I wish I could help you out, really I do. But you must realize that this dog is a valuable animal. I doubt if you could afford him, even if I was willing to sell him. I plan to show him. He's a prize dog, with even better lines than his mother. And she was a winner."

"What do you mean? Show him what?" Leo asked.

"Not what. Where. I'll show him at dog shows. Freckles is a purebred. A show winner. Once he settles down a little and reaches full growth, I'll be showing him all over the country."

"Will he like it?" Leo asked.

"He'll get used to it. Some dogs love it. They're real hams. Maybe Freckles will be like that."

Leo shook his head. It didn't sound like fun to him.

"So you see, I couldn't sell him to you. He's not an ordinary dog. But I'm grateful to you for taking such good care of him."

Mr. Edwards gave Leo's father some money to pay for the dog's food. Then he turned to Leo.

"You've done such a good job exercising Freckles and keeping his spirits up, I want to give you something to show my appreciation." He handed Leo a five-dollar bill.

Leo thanked the man, but he couldn't bring himself to smile.

He knelt down on the rug and hugged Chief

good-bye. The dog covered Leo's face with kisses, licking off the tears that rolled down his cheeks.

"Good dog. Good old dog," Leo said, grateful to Chief for licking his face. He didn't want the man to see his tears.

Mr. Edwards led the dog out to the car. Chief didn't seem sorry to be leaving, but as the car pulled away, he looked back at Leo with a puzzled expression, as if to say "Why aren't you coming?"

After they had left, Leo went up to his room and lay down on his bed. There was plenty of room now that Chief wasn't lying next to him.

I bet he'd rather live here with me than go to those dumb dog shows, Leo thought. Maybe he'll run away and come back here. But he knew in his heart that this would never happen.

After a while Leo stopped crying. He washed his face with cold water and went downstairs. His mother gave him a hug and so did his father. Even Eleanor said she was sorry that Chief had gone.

"We're getting a pizza for dinner," his mother said. "I think everyone could use a little cheering up around here tonight."

Leo was quiet during dinner. He was thinking

about Chief. After the dishes were rinsed and the table was cleared, he sat in the living room with his parents.

"Dad," he began. "Does a dog cost more than five dollars?"

"A fancy dog does. But a mixed breed, a mutt, probably doesn't cost much."

"Then that's what I'm going to do with this five dollars. Buy a new dog. A dog no one can take away. Okay?"

Both his parents nodded. "Yes, Leo. You've proved that you can take good care of one," his mother said.

"How about if we drive to the Animal Shelter on Saturday and see if there are any nice dogs looking for a home?" suggested his father.

Leo agreed. That sounded like a good idea.

That night Leo's bed felt wide and lonely with Chief missing. But it won't feel like this for long, Leo thought with a smile. Soon there would be a new dog by his side. And this time it would be his for keeps.

CHRISTINE McDONNELL, a bookbinder, sixth-grade teacher, and former librarian, is the author of many books for young readers, including *It's a Deal, Dogboy*, which is also about Leo and his friends, and *Ballet Bug*. Ms. McDonnell lives with her family in Brookline, Massachusetts.

G. Brian Karas is the illustrator of many children's books, including *Raising Sweetness, Cinder-Elly*, and *The Windy Day*. Mr. Karas lives with his family in Rhinebeck, New York.